For Neill, LaJon & Nilo —M.B.

For the mischief makers—Rumi, Tisa, Matin & Luca —S.M.

THIS IS A BORZOI BOOK PUBLISHED BY ALFRED A. KNOPF

Text copyright © 2021 by Matthew Burgess
Jacket art and interior illustrations copyright © 2021 by Shahrzad Maydani

All rights reserved. Published in the United States by Alfred A. Knopf, an imprint of
Random House Children's Books, a division of Penguin Random House LLC, New York.

Knopf, Borzoi Books, and the colophon are registered trademarks of Penguin Random House LLC.

Visit us on the Web! rhcbooks.com
Educators and librarians, for a variety of teaching tools, visit us at RHTeachersLibrarians.com

Library of Congress Cataloging-in-Publication Data
Names: Burgess, Matthew, author. | Maydani, Shahrzad, illustrator.
Title: Bird Boy / Matthew Burgess ; illustrated by Shahrzad Maydani.
Description: First edition. | New York : Alfred A. Knopf, [2021] |
Audience: Ages 3–7. | Audience: Grades K–1. | Summary: A new boy,
nicknamed Bird Boy by teasing classmates, enjoys imaginative flights as
various birds, gaining self-confidence and new friends.
Identifiers: LCCN 2019023104 (print) | LCCN 2019023105 (ebook) |
ISBN 978-1-9848-9377-2 (trade) | ISBN 978-1-9848-9378-9 (lib. bdg.) |
ISBN 978-1-9848-9379-6 (ebook)
Subjects: CYAC: Individuality—Fiction. | Birds—Fiction. |
Imagination—Fiction.
Classification: LCC PZ7.1.B8743 Bi 2021 (print) | LCC PZ7.1.B8743 (ebook)
| DDC [E]—dc23

The text of this book is set in 15-point Bembo.
The illustrations were created using watercolor, graphite, and colored pencil.
Book design by Elizabeth Tardiff

MANUFACTURED IN CHINA
July 2021
10 9 8 7 6 5 4 3 2 1
First Edition

Bird Boy

Matthew Burgess

Illustrated by Shahrzad Maydani

Alfred A. Knopf
New York

Nico was nervous
walking the path to class
    alone,
with a backpack full of stones.
        (That's how it felt.)

Nico was new,
so when everyone knew what to do
and where to go, he was left,
well, a little

        lost.

But there were other things to do
besides sports and standing
in huddles, whispering . . .

such as watching the insects
crossing a crack in the blacktop
like climbers over a mountain pass.

Or sitting in the grass like a statue

with the sun on your face,

until . . .

one bird hopped toward him,
waiting with shining eyes
and a side-curved head.

One bird, then two
(word had spread)
and flutter, swoop,
whistle, chirp . . .

That's how Nico
became known as

"BIRD BOY."

Nico knew when someone
was making fun of him—
and yes, it hurt his feelings.
But
he turned the name over in his mind
a few times

and smiled.

(It surprised him, too.)

"Bird Boy."

Soon Nico imagined himself
as an eagle soaring over a forest,

and a penguin
diving off an iceberg
into freezing
aquamarine
waters.

He became a hummingbird

hovering

amid the nectar-filled

flowers,

a pelican with wide-open wings,

cruising the edge of the coastline,

and a great
green-winged
macaw,

piercing the dusk

with her calls.

Not right away, but soon,
Nico made one friend,

then two.

They were drawn to Nico's kindness,

the wild flights of his imagination,

and the way he could be both a bird

and completely, delightfully himself.

Nico no longer felt nervous at recess
or walking the path to class alone.

In fact, sometimes he felt
just a few flaps away from . . .

liftoff.